Greenwich Council
Library & Information Service

Neatly fix library contact label here please
Mobile & Home Service
Tel: 020 8319 5875

Please return by the last date shown

Feb 2015

-- MAR 2015

-- NOV 2016

Vista
-- JAN 2017
STORKWAY
-- JUN 2017

Playwell 1
-- NOV 2017

Kidbrooke
RKP
-- NOV 2017

WWZ - MAR 2018

AB Moonlight
-- OCT 2018

WWCC
I- - MAY 2019

BBCn Bramble
-- JUN 2019

S-WILL -- OCT 2019

-- JAN 2020

-- NOV 2020

Thank You!

To renew, please contact any Greenwich library

Issue: 02 — Issue Date: 06.06.00 — Ref: RM.RBL.LIS

D1143704

To Claire, Elliott and Jack
K.G.
To the Sullivans
N.S.

A Red Fox Book 978 0 099 40467 5

Published by Random House Children's Books
61-63 Uxbridge Road, London WS 5SA

A division of The Random House Group Ltd
Addresses for companies within The Random House Group Limited
can be found at : www.randomhouse.co.uk/offices.htm

15 17 19 20 18 16

First published in Great Britain by The Bodley Head Children's Books 2000

Red Fox edition 2001

Printed and bound in Singapore

THE RANDOM HOUSE GROUP Limited Reg. No. 954009

www.kidsatrandomhouse.co.uk

Eat Your Peas

Kes Gray & Nick Sharratt

RED FOX

It was dinner time again and Daisy just knew what her mum was going to say, before she even said it.
"Eat your peas," said Mum.

Daisy looked down at the little green balls
that were ganging up on her plate.
"I don't like peas," said Daisy.

Mum sighed one of her usual sighs. "If you eat your peas, you can have some pudding," said Mum.

"I don't like peas," said Daisy.

"If you eat your peas, you can have some pudding and  you can stay up for an extra half hour."

"I don't like peas," said Daisy.

"If you eat your peas, you can have some pudding,  stay up for an extra half hour and you can skip your bath."

"I don't like peas," said Daisy.

"If you eat your peas, you can have ten puddings,

 stay up really late, you don't have to wash for

two whole months and I'll buy

you a new bike."

"I don't like peas," said Daisy.

"If you eat your peas, you can have 48 puddings, stay up past midnight, you never have to wash again, I'll buy you two new bikes and a baby elephant."

"I don't like peas," said Daisy.

"If you eat your peas, you can have 100 puddings,

you can go to bed when you want, wash when you want,

do what you want when you want,

I'll buy you ten new bikes,

two pet elephants,   three zebras,   a penguin

and a chocolate factory."

"I don't like peas," said Daisy.

 "If you eat your peas, I'll buy you a supermarket stacked full of puddings,  you never have to go to bed again ever, or school  again, you never have to wash, or brush your hair, or clean your shoes,  or tidy your bedroom,

I'll buy you a bike shop, a zoo, ten chocolate factories,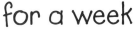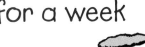

I'll take you to Superland for a week and you can have your very own space rocket with double retro laser blammers."

"If you eat your peas, I'll buy you every supermarket, sweet shop, toy shop and bike shop in the world, seventeen swimming pools, you never have to go to bed again, or go to school, or wash, or brush your hair or clean your shoes, or clean your teeth, or clean your hamster out, or tidy your bedroom, or put the videos in yourself, or get dressed,

I'll buy you Africa and ninety two chocolate factories, we'll move to Superland, you can have all the space rockets you want, I'll buy you the earth, the moon, the stars, the sun and... and... and...

...and a new fluffy pencil case!"

"You really want me to eat my peas, don't you?" said Daisy.
"Yes," said Mum.

"I'll eat *my* peas if you eat *your* Brussels," said Daisy.

Mum looked down at her own plate
and her bottom lip began to wobble.
"But I don't like Brussels," said Mum.

"But we both like pudding!"

Really, Really
Kes Gray & Nick Sharratt

You Do!
Kes Gray & Nick Sharratt

Yuk!
Kes Gray & Nick Sharratt

006 and a Bit
Kes Gray & Nick Sharratt

With a free DAISY SPY KIT!

Come and play with Daisy at
Daisy Club
Kes Gray & Nick Sharratt
MEET DAISY · FUN STUFF · DAISY CLUB · GROWN-UPS · DAISY SHOP · DAISY BLOOM
www.daisyclub.co.uk

Kes Gray
Nick Sharratt
Double Trouble
Now with 8 pages of fun activities!

Tiger Ways
Kes Gray & Nick Sharratt

With free DAISY FINGER PUPPET!

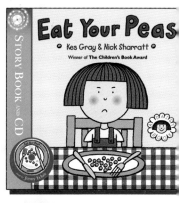

Eat Your Peas
Kes Gray & Nick Sharratt
Winner of The Children's Book Award
STORY BOOK AND CD

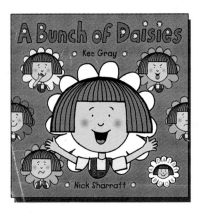

A Bunch of Daisies
Kes Gray
Nick Sharratt

DAISY and the TROUBLE with LIFE
by Kes Gray
With a free DAISY BOOKMARK

DAISY and the TROUBLE with ZOOS
by Kes Gray
free Daisy BOOKMARK inside!

DAISY and the TROUBLE with GIANTS
by Kes Gray
Free Daisy BOOKMARK inside!

Accidentally on Purpose
A split-page book with ninety naughty mix-ups!
Kes Gray & Nick Sharratt

New longer Daisy story books!